ARTHUR HOWARD

HoodwinKeD

Harcourt, Inc.
San Diego   New York   London

E
HOW

www.harcourt.com

Library of Congress Cataloging-in-Publication Data
Howard, Arthur.
Hoodwinked/Arthur Howard.
p.   cm.
Summary: A young witch searches for a creepy pet.
[1. Pets—Fiction.   2. Witches—Fiction.]   I. Title.
PZ7.H8283Ho   2001
[E]—dc21   00-8318
ISBN 0-15-202656-8

First edition
H G F E D C B A
Manufactured in China

The display type was created by Judythe Sieck.
The text type was set in Celestia Antiqua.
Color separations by Colourscan Co. Pte. Ltd., Singapore
Manufactured by South China Printing Company, Ltd., China
This book was printed on totally chlorine-free Nymolla Matte Art paper.
Production supervision by Sandra Grebenar and Pascha Gerlinger
Designed by Arthur Howard and Judythe Sieck

For Rachel, Rebecca, and Sophia

Mitzi liked creepy things.

Creepy bedroom slippers.
Creepy breakfast cereal.

Creepy relatives.

So, naturally, when she decided to get a pet, she wanted the creepiest pet possible.

She couldn't go to the local pet shop—it only had cute, cuddly pets. Instead, she hopped on her broomstick and flew to a place called Cackle & Company.

"May I help you?" asked the shop lady. She had a short green nose and long blue teeth. Mitzi liked her right away.

"I want a pet," she said. "Something really, really creepy."

The lady showed her snakes that slithered,
worms that squirmed,

and a toad that was covered in slime.
"I'll take the toad," said Mitzi.

Mumps—that's what Mitzi named the toad—was wonderfully creepy. But he wasn't much of a pet. When Mitzi hunted ghosts in the attic, Mumps ate bugs. When Mitzi watched a creature feature on TV, Mumps ate bugs.

When Mitzi told him her deepest, darkest secrets,
Mumps didn't even look at her. He just ate bugs.

Mitzi flew back to the shop.

"I want another pet," she said. "Something a little less buggy."

The lady showed her a cage full of owls, a tank full of eels,

and a room full of bats.

"Those bats are the creepiest things I've ever seen," said Mitzi. "I'll take two."

She named the bats Toothache and Earwax.

"I couldn't ask for anything creepier," Mitzi kept telling herself.

But all the bats did was hang around with each other.

Mitzi hurried back to the shop.
"I want another pet," she said. "Something a bit less batty."
"I have just the thing...," said the lady.

"WARTHOGS!"
"Hmm," said Mitzi.
"Let me think it over."

As she flew home, Mitzi wondered if she'd ever find a pet that was right for her.

All of her creepy relatives had pets. Uncle Churly had piranhas. Aunt Malice had a crocodile. Even Madam Vex had a pet, though no one was quite sure what it was.

Everyone has a pet, Mitzi thought. *Except me.*

But things that are nearly magical happen all the time—especially to witches. And sure enough, the very next day there was a scratch, scratch, scratching at the back door.

"What could that be?" Mitzi wondered.

When she opened the door, she saw a tiny little kitten.

"Ugh," said Mitzi. "You're cute."

The kitten gazed up at her and meowed a tiny little meow.

"You're worse than cute," Mitzi muttered. "You're adorable."

Still, it was beginning to rain, so Mitzi let the kitten in. "You can stay one night," she said. "But only one. You're simply not creepy enough."

But that night when Mitzi hunted ghosts in the attic,
the kitten prowled by her side.

When Mitzi watched a creature feature on TV, the kitten purred on her lap. And at bedtime when she told him her deepest, darkest secrets, the kitten licked her chin.

Mitzi had finally found a pet. She named him Hoodwink, and strange as it seems, she didn't mind one bit that he was adorable.

"After all," she said, "looks aren't everything."

And even her creepy relatives had to agree.